Praise for *Free Bird*

"Kids and parents will cheer for Flaco as he chases adventure and follows his dreams. A chance to see the world through the eyes of an owl, this book provides kids with an inspiring glimpse into the emotional lives of animals and an important reminder that hope, and freedom are universal themes for us all."—**Gene Baur**, president and co-founder, Farm Sanctuary

"Combine reverence for an owl who showed the world that we *all* yearn for freedom, a parent's wise and encouraging voice, and a devotion to animal advocacy, and you've got a gem of a book. It's impossible not to fall in love with Flaco, and in doing so, to expand one's heart toward *all* captive animals who long to be free."—**Kathy Stevens**, founder, Catskill Animal Sanctuary

"*Free Bird: Flaco the Owl's Dreams Take Flight* is a captivating children's book that tells the inspiring tale of Flaco, an owl who finds freedom in the bustling city of New York. Its uplifting message weaves in the plight of animals in captivity and their dream to be free. Combined with its stunning illustrations, Flaco's journey will inspire children to dream big and be brave enough to reach for the stars."—**Kathleen Schatzmann**, strategic legislative affairs manager, Animal Legal Defense Fund

"*Free Bird: Flaco the Owl's Dreams Take Flight* does an extraordinary job of capturing how we all have dreams—whether you're a child or a nonhuman animal—and how important it is to fulfill these dreams. As someone who works every day to help animals, I am moved by the care and respect given to Flaco's yearning for freedom. Flaco's dream became a reality, and I am so excited to imagine the book in the hands of young readers who will hopefully learn from Flaco's incredible story."—**Elizabeth Stein, Esq.**, litigation director, The Nonhuman Rights Project

FREE BIRD

Flaco the Owl's Dreams Take Flight

By Christine Mott
Illustrations by Ofra Layla Isler

Lantern Publishing & Media • Woodstock and Brooklyn, NY

2025
Lantern Publishing & Media
PO Box 1350
Woodstock, NY 12498
www.lanternpm.org

Printed in the United States of America

Library of Congress Cataloging-in-Publication Data is available upon request.

For Flaco: May your struggle for freedom open the eyes of the world to the suffering of animals everywhere.

To my daughters, Laila and Eva: May you lead the next generation of animal advocates.

To my husband, Amir: I am grateful for your love and support.

Half of the proceeds from this book will be donated to the Wild Bird Fund, a 501(c)(3) non-profit that rehabilitates sick, injured and orphaned wildlife and releases them back to the wilds of New York City.

Have you ever had a dream so big, so crazy, so amazing, that you felt like it could never come true?

I'm Flaco the owl. I know all about big dreams—mine were as big as the sky!

After all, this is New York, the City of Dreams.

Some people say that a person without a dream is like a bird who can't fly. Well, my dream was to soar free and live a life of my own.

For my whole life, I held onto my dream. Sometimes it felt too hard, too scary, too impossible. But I didn't give up.

Here is my story . . .

One day I looked up at the sky through the metal fence of my cage at the zoo. Sparrows and pigeons flew by, chirping happily, free in the sky. Sometimes they stopped to chat with me.

How I wished to join them—to stretch my wings in the air, to go on adventures and be wild. But all my life I lived alone inside four walls that separated me from the world. Each day, I stared at a painted mural of the mountains and imagined what it must be like to soar so high.

What would it feel like to perch on a real treetop? People marvel that I'm the biggest owl in the world but I never even had the chance to fly. Didn't they know my dream was to sail across the sky?

One night, everything would change. A little sparrow landed on the wire fence of my cage—she popped her head inside to greet me. "Hello!—are you joining us this evening?"

"What do you mean?" I asked as my orange eyes looked up curiously. To my amazement, I saw a hole in the fence. It opened up to the sky like a doorway to a grand adventure!

But where would I go?
What would I find?
Where would I sleep?
What would I eat?

I'd never find out unless I tried. I crawled to the hole and slowly climbed out. For the first time in my life, I was on the outside of the fence. Using all of my might, I heaved my wings open and flew into the night sky.

I was free! I hooted in excitement as I soared into the sky. Sparrows chirped their encouragement! "Go Flaco, Go!"

The other animals couldn't believe their eyes. "How do you like me now?" I hooted. Soon everyone was cheering me on. "Fly free, Flaco!" I left my old life behind and I never looked back.

These wings were made for flying!
And boy do I love soaring in the sky!
At first it was tricky.

My wings were a little wobbly because I never had the chance to fly before. But I had to keep trying.

Some of the sparrows gave me flying lessons. Every day, I was a little stronger and I could fly a little bit farther. After some practice, you'd think I was born flying!

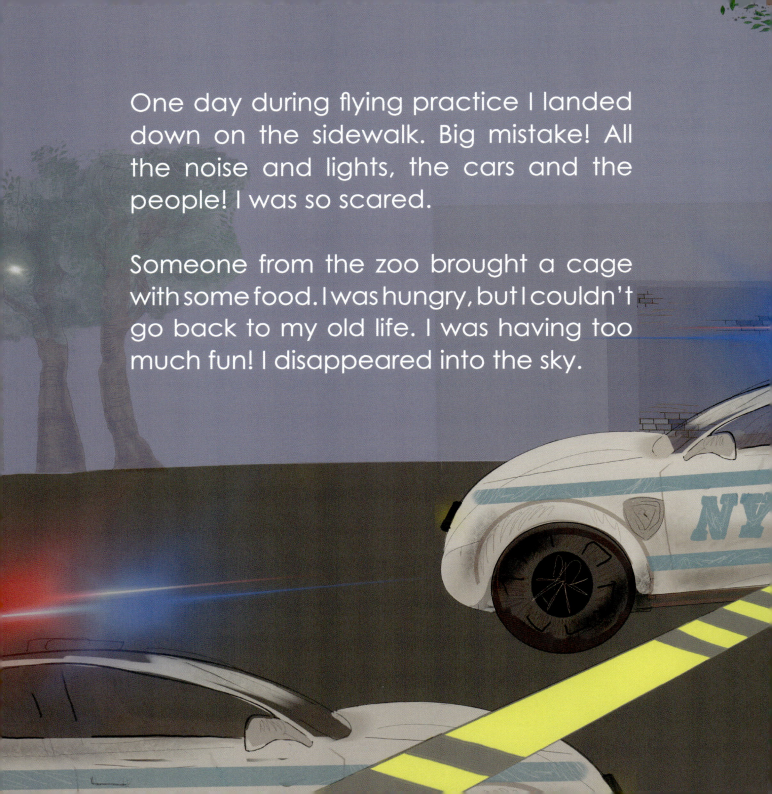

One day during flying practice I landed down on the sidewalk. Big mistake! All the noise and lights, the cars and the people! I was so scared.

Someone from the zoo brought a cage with some food. I was hungry, but I couldn't go back to my old life. I was having too much fun! I disappeared into the sky.

My belly grumbled. I hadn't eaten anything since I made my escape. The sparrows told me there was plenty of food in the park. I listened, I watched and I finally caught my very own dinner! Who says an old owl can't learn new tricks?!

For so long my world was just a tiny cage, but now I am king of the city skies! I chase adventure and feel my feathers glide across the night air.

Some people said my dream was too big, but I've proved them all wrong. I learn as I go. I'm doing things I've never done before. If I can make it here, I can make it anywhere!

There is so much to explore in this city. It's a real hoot!

I've visited the giant green lady in the middle of the river . . .

Sampled some delicious treats . . .

Enjoyed some window shopping . . .

Watched a ballgame . . .

Learned about art . . .

Checked out NYC real estate . . .

Attended some fancy parties.

But my favorite place is the park where I've met many friends.

Like Freddy the fox who showed me the best places to find dinner.

Tilda the turtle entertains me with stories of her underwater adventures.

Rebekah the raccoon shares secret hiding spots.

Bernard the bat shares his flying expertise.

Of course in the big city not everyone is friendly, you can't be too careful!

I've fought off a red tailed hawk when he landed in my favorite tree and defended myself against a pack of crows and some blue jays.

I've even outsmarted all those pesky traps from the zoo. I'm so happy out here—as free as. . . . Well as free as a bird should be!

Now I'm living my dreams—only the sky is my limit!

Three hoots for freedom!

For an old owl like me it's been quite a fun ride! Looking back at my life, some people say I should have just stayed at the zoo. Well if you were me, what would you do? My days of freedom and adventure have been the best times of my life! Even now my spirit is still flying free and I'll never ever stop!

We owls have a reputation for wisdom, so let me pass on my advice to you: Dream big dreams. Be determined, be brave, be adventurous and believe in yourself. Any dream needs a plan, there's the *"how"* and the *"when."* But the most important part of it is the *"WHOOO"*—and that *"who"* is you.

Fun Facts About Owls!

🦉 There are over 200 owl species in the world. Flaco was a Eurasian Eagle Owl, the largest species of owl with a wingspan of over 6 feet wide! That's bigger than the height of the average adult human! The world's tiniest owl is the Pygmy Owl, which can be as small as a person's hand!

🦉 Most owls are nocturnal (active at night), but some owl species are crepuscular (active in the twilight hours of dawn and dusk) and diurnal (active in the daytime). Nocturnal owls are more likely to have dark eyes while crepuscular and diurnal owls are more likely to have orange or yellow eyes.

🦉 Owls have super eyes! Unlike most birds, owls have front-facing eyes that provide them with 3-D vision. Owls have night vision that is 35 to 100 times better than human night vision. Their eyes are giant in proportion to their body size, making up 5% of their body weight (compare that to human eyes which are 0.0003% of an adult's body weight). If human eyes were the same proportion as owl eyes, they would be the size of grapefruits!

🦉 An owl's neck can rotate 270 degrees (three quarters of a full circle) to look directly backwards and 90 degrees up and down, even upside down!

🦉 Owls have three eyelids! The upper eyelid is for blinking, the lower eyelid is for sleeping and the third eyelid is a transparent lid that they can close to protect their eyes from injury and dirt while flying.

🦉 Owls have outstanding hearing and can hear up to 10 times better than humans! Owls have flat faces that funnel sound to their ears, and one ear that is bigger and higher than the other to help them hear from all directions.

🦉 The color and pattern of owls' feathers allows them to hide in their surroundings and can even change with the seasons. Owl feathers have rough edges (like the teeth of a comb) that allow them to fly silently. Many owls have tufts of feathers on the top of their heads which are used to indicate an owl's moods, such as excitement, fear and anger.

About the Author

Christine Mott is an attorney and animal advocate with over 15 years of experience leading legal and policy efforts to protect animals. Christine is a former Chair of the Animal Law Committee of the NYC Bar Association and has served on the boards of various animal advocacy organizations. Christine received her J.D. from NYU Law and her B.A. from Smith College and is a graduate of Emma Willard School. Christine's work has been featured in the New York Times and various media. A native New Yorker, Christine lives in Southern California with her husband, two daughters, a dog and two guinea pigs (all rescues). Learn more about Christine at www.christinemott.com.

About the Illustrator

Ofra Layla Isler is a California-based artist, animal advocate, and the founder of Art in Rescue, which honors the work of animal rescue through detailed hand drawn art. Inspired by the beautiful animals who are given second chances to live a life in peace, she brings her passion for art and animal rights together through this endeavor. Ofra has worked with various animal advocacy and conservation organizations. She enjoys hiking and exploring Sonoma County before coming home to her two rescue kitties.

About the Publisher

Lantern Publishing & Media was founded in 2020 to follow and expand on the legacy of Lantern Books—a publishing company started in 1999 on the principles of living with a greater depth and commitment to the preservation of the natural world. Like its predecessor, Lantern Publishing & Media produces books on animal advocacy, veganism, religion, social justice, humane education, psychology, family therapy, and recovery. Lantern is dedicated to printing in the United States on recycled paper and saving resources in our day-to-day operations. Our titles are also available as ebooks and audiobooks.

To catch up on Lantern's publishing program, visit us at www.lanternpm.org.

facebook.com/lanternpm
instagram.com/lanternpm
tiktok.com/@lanternpmofficial